HERCULES, the Gentle Giant

HERCULES, the Gentle Giant

by Nina Schneider

Pictures by Tomie de Paola

HAWTHORN BOOKS, INC. • PUBLISHERS • NEW YORK

for Steve, my gentle giant

First Edition: 1969

HERCULES, the Gentle Giant

Once upon a time, in a walled city by the sea, lived a boy named Hercules. Even when he was a baby, Hercules could do things a grownup found too difficult.

Hercules was big, and he kept growing bigger. He grew so fast that his mother, Alcmena, had a hard time keeping him in clothes that fit. She would weave a beautiful robe with large gold designs around the hem, and before it was quite finished, Hercules had grown another bit and she had to weave another piece to make it longer.

Every day he grew bigger and stronger and wider and longer. He burst his belts and snapped his sandal buckles and even had to give up wearing undershirts altogether.

He outgrew his bed, he outgrew the chairs, he had to stoop way down when he came indoors. Of course he was too tall for school. But anyway he didn't care for books and making speeches. So he stayed around home and was a giant.

He was shy with other people and the sky
was comfortably high. He got into the habit
of being outdoors, which is a joyous habit
indeed. He learned to swim like a fish, run like a
deer, walk swiftly and silently as an elephant
(which is very swift and silent, as you know).
He also learned to lie still as a snail in the sun.
Most of all, young Hercules loved to lie under the
trees and watch for falling feathers.

"How lovely a house would be if the roof
was thatched with feathers," he often thought.
So he picked up feathers and kept them, just
in case. He also collected colored pebbles,
driftwood, strange shells, and such.

He was cheerful about chores, and his mother often said, "He is a good boy, my little giant."

When she needed some firewood, he would go stomping and clomping through the woods to find a dry dead tree. He could pull it up, lift it to his shoulders, and carry it to the back door without even a grunt. There he would break it up into convenient sizes as you might break a twig or a matchstick.

His mother loved Hercules very much because he was her son, and because he was gentle and kind, though he was strong and could have bullied anyone. She talked about *her* Hercules to the neighbors in the market place, as mothers do. In the evening the neighbors told their husbands about Hercules. It was not long before everyone in the city knew about Hercules, the Gentle Giant, who was willing to pull out a tree or move a boulder, or do any odd job like that to oblige a neighbor.

Soon the king heard of him, too.

Now the king was a coward, and he was round and so fat he couldn't find his feet. And what is more, he wanted to be the first, *and* the biggest, *and* the best, *and* the smartest, *and* the most famous, *and* to have the largest share.

Instead of doing brave deeds himself, the king spent his time being cranky and making faces and complaining in a high whining voice, even though he had seven castles, one for each day in the week. And each castle had pastry cooks, picture books, and candy and ice cream. He had fields full of flowers, and a huge herd of pretty red and white cows, and so many bags of gold and jewels that he had to leapfrog over them to get to the golden throne.

"I don't believe there is such a one as Hercules," the king said to his seven wise men, "and anyway, I don't like him."

All the seven wise men nodded their heads most wisely, because they were paid to do just that.

Well, it happened in this city that a fierce, huge, roaring, hunting lion became interested in the sheep– much too interested.

You see, right outside the city wall there was a large grassy meadow where the shepherds and shepherdesses liked to take their sheep to graze.

They led the animals carefully down through the city gates and then, while the flocks safely nibbled the green grass, there would be time to sit by the stream. The boys played their pipes and sang. The girls made daisy chains and danced.

Then this fierce, huge, roaring, hunting lion came along and spoiled all the fun. He rushed out of the brush and, with a loud roar that frightened all the poor sheep and shepherds, the fierce beast pounced on a sheep and carried it off.

This of course made everyone unhappy, except the lion.

Hunters came to help. They stood on the high city wall and waited until the lion came back. They shot their arrows at him. The guards jumped up and down and shouted, "Get him, get him!" But the lion only roared more loudly and paid no attention to the arrows that pierced his sides.

This was of course very discouraging to the
hunters. After all, if the lion didn't run away
like a proper lion when he was shot at, why,
what could they do? Only try again. And they
tried and tried, again and again, until the
lion was so full of arrows he looked like a
porcupine or a target.

At last they realized it was *no use*. And they said, "Let us go to the king. He ought to take care of *special business*."

So early Monday morning they went to the cowardly fat king—two hunters, two horses, two shepherds, two shepherdesses, and two sheep. The two horses carried the hunters. The two hunters carried their bows and arrows. The two shepherds carried their pipes. The two shepherdesses carried a wilted daisy chain. (They had been so busy about the lion they hadn't been able to weave a fresh chain.) And the two sheep just came along, their white heads hanging sadly and their red tongues hanging out. It was a sad group.

When the king heard the noise, he was frightened.
He thought he had better get out of the throne room of the
Monday palace. But a servant ran to the window and
said, "Everything is safe."

When the people told the little fat king their story, he said at once, "Why don't you get this Hercules fellow you've been telling me about? You don't expect *me* to get off my throne to kill a lion. I could, of course, kill him but I don't want to."

The seven wise men were busy nodding their heads and saying, "He could, he could kill the lion." So they were of no help at all.

The two horses, the two hunters, the two shepherds, the two sheperdesses, and the two sheep turned about and went to the door. Just as they reached it, the king shouted, "I order Hercules to kill the lion and bring his skin to my Tuesday palace tomorrow!"

And each of the seven wise men said in turn, "To the Tuesday palace, tomorrow."

So the sad group went to the place where Hercules lay watching for falling feathers.

Hercules heard them coming and got up to greet them, although he had just seen a red feather falling and wanted to get it very much.

"What can I do for you, good neighbors?" he asked politely. They told him of their troubles with the lion and the king.

"I'll try to get him for you, the lion, I mean," said Hercules, bravely.

His mother came out and heard the story, too. She said, "Don't you think, Hercules, you're a little young to go chasing lions?"

"Don't worry, Mother. I am swifter than a lion and stronger than an ox," he said, modestly.

"But still you're young for lion-hunting," said his mother.

"That is true, but I'm very big and strong," said Hercules.

"That is certainly true, too," agreed Alcmena. "I suppose you must go, my boy."

So early the next morning Hercules went up to the city wall.

All the most interested people came, too: the hunters, the shepherds, the housewives, the young girls with shining faces, and *all* the little boys in the city. Hercules, armed with a club, sat on the edge of the wall and waited, swinging his legs and whistling.

By and by, at his breakfast time, the lion started out of the woods. The air was filled with his roaring. Hercules leaped from the high wall and walked swiftly and silently toward the lion. When the lion saw him he was surprised. He just stood there with his mouth open in the middle of a roar.

It was simple after that.

Hercules pushed his club way down into the lion's throat, then grabbed him by the tail and swung him around and around and around and around, and then dropped him on his head. And that was the end of the lion.

Everyone shouted, "Hurrah, hurrah, for hero Hercules!" The little boys shouted, loudest of all, "Hurrah, hurrah, for Hercules!"

It was still early, so the women and the girls took what had been the lion and made a grand lion costume for Hercules. It fitted him perfectly. Hercules bowed and said, "Thank you," and they giggled and said, "Oh, thank *you*."

Then Hercules put the lion's head in front of his face, like a mask, and went toward the Tuesday palace. The people followed him, still shouting.

When the cowardly king heard the tremendous noise, he began to tremble and quake, to shiver and shake, like a cold custard cake.

Hercules knocked at the door with a great bang! bang!

The king dived in back of his golden throne and his voice went down to his belly like water emptying down the bathtub drain. "Come in," he whispered, as he tried to shout.

Hercules didn't hear him, so he knocked at the palace door with an even louder bang! bang!

The servant at the door and the one at the window said, "A lion, Your Majesty."

The king didn't answer this time. Holding his crown
with one hand and his belly with the other, he went
running down the hall.

Hercules opened the door and marched in, with all
the people following him. When he saw the king running
away he leaped after him over the bags of treasure. In two
seconds he caught up with him.

Hercules laughed and laughed, and took off his lion mask. When the king saw that it was only Hercules, he stood up as straight as a round king can stand and said, in a whisper and a shout, "I wasn't running away. I WAS GOING FOR A DRINK."

The seven wise men nodded quickly, "YES! YES! HE WAS GOING FOR A DRINK."

Then the king climbed back on to his Tuesday throne. He sent everyone away. He wanted to be alone and sulk.

Everyone was glad to leave. They went back to the green meadow and had the most wonderful, beautiful picnic. Hercules wore his new lion costume.

The king watched from the window and saw the fun. At last he decided to go out anyway.

The shepherds played their pipes and sang in low, sweet tones. The girls made daisy chains and danced around Hercules, who blushed because he was shy. The sheep slept peacefully in a big circle around their hero's party.

Early in the evening, Hercules left the singing and dancing and went home to his favorite spot under the open sky to wait for falling feathers. And that is where he usually stayed whenever he was not doing great deeds.